WAIT TILL THE MOON IS FULL

by

Margaret Wise Brown

pictures by

Garth Williams

HarperCollins*Publishers*

Wait Till the Moon Is Full

Copyright, 1948, by Margaret Wise Brown

Text copyright renewed 1976 by Roberta Brown Rauch

Pictures copyright renewed 1976 by Garth Williams

Printed in Mexico. All rights reserved.

ISBN 0-06-020800-7

ISBN 0-06-020801-5 (lib. bdg.)

ISBN 0-06-443222-X (pbk.)

LC Number 48-9278

ONCE upon a time in the dark of the moon
there was a little raccoon.

He lived down in a big warm chestnut tree
with his mother — who was also a raccoon.

This little raccoon wanted to see the night. He had seen the day.

So he said to his mother, "I want to go out in the woods and see the night."

But his mother said, "Wait."

"Wait till the moon is full." So he waited, deep in his warm little home under the chestnut tree.

Above him he could hear the night wind rustling above his head and clicking the black branches. He couldn't see out, but he could hear out.

He heard a bird fall out of its nest and fly away.

He heard owls hooting in the trees and a big silence all around.

And he said to his mother, "I want to know an owl."

But his mother said, "Wait. Wait till the moon is full."

"Outside it is very dark," said his mother.

"How dark is the dark?" murmured the little raccoon, as he clung to his mother's warm side.

"Very dark," whispered his mother.

"Let me go out and look at the dark," whispered the little raccoon.

"Wait," whispered his mother. "Wait till the moon is full."

"How dark is the dark tonight?" asked the little raccoon.

"Not so dark," said his mother. "There is a new moon tonight, thin as the curve of a raccoon's whisker in the sky above the tree tops."

"Can I see it?" asked the little raccoon.

"No," said his mother. "You must wait. Wait till the moon is full."

"How big is the night?" asked the little raccoon.

"Very big," said his mother.

"How big is Big?" asked the little raccoon.

"Wait," said his mother. "Wait till the moon is full."

So he waited and grew quietly fat and wondered.

He washed his paws and combed his whiskers, and time passed.

"How big is the moon tonight?" asked the little raccoon.

"A half moon," said his mother. "Big as the curve of a raccoon's ear."

"Where is it?" asked the little raccoon.

"Half way up the sky," said his mother.

"I want to see it," said the little raccoon.

"Wait," said his mother. "Wait till the moon is full."

And his mother began to sing. She sang a raccoon song about the Night and the Moon.

Soft in the night
In the bright moonlight
Rabbits run all through the night
And never bump into each other
In the Full of the Moon
When the Moon is Full.

And the cat and the cow
And the fish and bull
Dance an animal dance
When the moon is full
With the owl and the squirrel
And the skunk and the gull.

And a little bird cries
From over the hill.
"Whip poor Will,
Whip poor Will."
My little raccoon
Be still, be still
And wait till the moon is full.

"Does everyone sleep at night?" asked the little raccoon.

"No," said his mother, "not everyone."

"Who doesn't?" asked the little raccoon.

"All things that love the night," said his mother. "Wait till the moon is full."

"Is the moon a rabbit?" asked the little raccoon.

"No," said his mother. "The moon is a moon. A big round golden moon."

"Will I see it soon?"

"Wait," said his mother. "Wait till the moon is full."

"Is the night blue or black or red or white?" asked the little raccoon all at once.

And because his mother couldn't answer all his questions all at once, she sang him another song.

When the moon has turned its back
Then the night is big and black,
Dark, Dark in the dark of the moon.

But when the moon is thin and new
Then you'll see the night turn blue,
Blue, Blue when the moon is new.

Long after rabbits are safe in bed
Then the moon sets low and red,
Red, Red when the moon is low.

But wait, wait till the bright moonlight
Bursts on the night all silvery white,
Wait till the moon is full.

"I want to see a bird fall out of his nest and fly away in the moonlight," said the little raccoon.

"Wait," said his mother. "Wait till the moon is full."

"And find another little raccoon to play with."

"Wait," said his mother. "Wait till the moon is full."

So one day the little raccoon looked up at his mother and said, "See here, my big warm mother, can I go now — out in the woods to see the night?"

And his mother said,

"If you want to go out in the woods
and see the night
and know an owl
and how dark is the dark
and see the moon
and how big is the night
and listen to the Whip poor Will
and stay up all night
and sleep all day
and see that the moon isn't a rabbit
and what color is the night
and see a bird fall out of his nest
and fly away in the moonlight
and find another little raccoon to play with,
off you go, for —

the moon is full."